Eyeball

D1589864

Magut the Alien

written by

Ian MacDonald

Illustrated by Charlie Clough

First published
January 06 in Great Britain by

Educational Printing Services Limited
Albion Mill, Water Street, Great Harwood, Blackburn BB6 7QR
Telephone: (01254) 882080   Fax: (01254) 882010
e-mail: enquiries@eprint.co.uk   web site: www.eprint.co.uk

ISBN 1 904904-59-9

Contents

Eyeball Soup

1	Green Soup	1
2	The Iron Gates	13
3	Tin Can Alley	21
4	Von Straub	26
5	"Awake, my Beauties!"	32
6	Robot Attack!	36

Magut the Alien

1	Aliens in my Shed	49
2	"Greetings Earthchild!"	53
3	Magut	57
4	New Shoes	61
5	Happy Birthday!	68
6	Life on Mars	76

Eyeball Soup

Chapter 1
Green Soup

Owen crossed over the road toward the great iron gates.

"Come on, Owen," shouted Chaz. "Let's get home."

"The bus will be here any minute!" yelled Freddie.

Owen was going on about the factory again. There was just something about it.

For a start, no one ever went in and no one ever came out. And what did the factory make anyway?

No one knew. But then again, no one cared. Not even his best friends would listen.

"You're bonkers, Owen," laughed Chaz, bouncing a tennis ball on the pavement.

"Why don't you just give it a rest?" jeered Freddie.

"But I just know there's something weird about the place. It gives me the creeps just walking past it."

"Don't walk past it then," said Chaz.

"Shut your eyes," said Freddie, doing an impression of someone blindfolded.

But Owen wasn't listening. This time he was going to find out what was inside.

Owen stood in the gateway staring hard at the rows of dark windows; the chimney at the far end continued to pour silent smoke into the blank sky.

And then it happened.

From somewhere in the darkness came the sound of a door shutting. And, from the shadows something came rolling towards him, clanking across the grey stone, and stopped right by his foot.

It was a tin can.

. . . .

On the bus home Owen took the can out of his school bag, turning it over in his hand.

"I told you there was something, didn't I?"

"So what! It's just an old tin can," said Chaz. "What's so special about that?"

"But look," said Owen, "it's not the same as the ones in the shops is it?"

It was true. It was the same shape and size as any tin can. But the label was not like anything Owen had seen before. It was plain black and, printed in green letters were just two words:

GREEN SOUP

"Green soup! Yuk!" said Chaz.

"It's probably full of cabbage an' brussel-sprouts and stuff like that."

Freddie put two fingers in his mouth and pretended to be sick.

"Well, meet me at the den tonight and we'll open it together," said Owen. "Then you'll see."

But inside he wasn't so sure. Perhaps it was just soup. Maybe the factory was nothing special. Maybe it was just all in his imagination.

. . . .

Before he could meet his mates at the den there was shopping to be done.

"Pass me a can of soup will you, dear?" said Mum.

"Neeaouw! Alien spaceships attacking! Guns away!"

Owen wandered over to the stack of cans, his hand swooping in ready to dock with the space-station. He took hold of the nearest can and tugged.

There was a crashing, tumbling sound and Owen stood there, soup cans covering his feet.

One or two shoppers peered round to look. A shop assistant in a green overall came over and began to pick up the cans. "That's a good trick," she said, crossly.

"Owen," sighed his mum. "How many times do I have to tell you not to take the bottom one?"

"Sorry," mumbled Owen.

. . . .

When he got to the den they were all waiting.

"This is a waste of time, there's football on the telly," grumbled Chaz.

"Come on then, let's get it over with."

The den was their hide-out. It was made out of an old fence panel, some bits of hardboard and other odds and ends. An assortment of old boxes provided chairs and a table.

Owen put the tin can down on the table and took the can-opener from his pocket that he had borrowed from home.

"Go on then, hurry up," said Chaz. "I bet Rovers are 2-nil up by now."

Owen leaned forward and clamped the opener over the edge and began to wind. There was a faint hiss.

"Pooh, what a pong!" gasped Freddie, moving away slightly.

Owen ignored him and carried on turning until a circle of tin fell away. He turned the can upside down.

A thick, green liquid oozed out forming a small mountain in the middle of the table.

"It's just soup," said Chaz.

"Big deal!" said Freddie.

Slowly, the liquid slid apart spreading wetly across the table top.

And there, in the middle of the green mess, was a metal ball.

And then the metal ball whirred . . . peeled back two folds of metallic skin . . . and blinked!

Chapter 2
The Iron Gates

In Science they were making electric circuits.

"Attach the wires to the battery and then see if you can make a switch from a couple of paper clips," Old Potts was saying. The three boys sat at the back whispering.

"What have you done with it?"

"It's in my pencil case."

"What!?"

"I couldn't think of anywhere else!"

"You must be nuts! It'll stink the place out."

Owen unzipped the pencil case and put the metal ball on the table. Since yesterday evening the metal ball had refused to do anything. No whirring sounds. No opening eyelids. But it had definitely looked at them yesterday. An eye looking out of a metal ball.

"What have you got there?"

It was old Potts.

"Nothing, Sir," spluttered Owen.

"It's er . . . just a marble, Sir," said Freddie, trying to rescue the situation.

Potts picked it up. "Looks more like a ball bearing to me," he said.

"A ball bearing, Sir?"

"It's something used in factories that make machine parts, wheels and things like that. They cut down friction, help things to move more smoothly. Now, perhaps you'll get on with your circuit, you three . . . that is, if you can spare your valuable time!"

"Phew! That was close," said Freddie, when Potts had gone.

"Well at least we know what it is now," said Chaz.

"Of course we don't," snapped Owen.

"It's obviously not a ball bearing. It's an eye. The point is, what does it belong to? I'm going back tonight to find out."

"You're mad!"

"Are you coming? Or are you a scaredy cat?" said Owen.

"Of course not," replied Freddie. "Just name the time and we'll be there."

"Will we?" spluttered Chaz.

. . . .

It was dark when the three friends met outside the great iron gates. The moon blinked from behind a cloud outlining the dark shapes of the buildings.

"Just a quick look, you said. And then we go back home, right?"

"We'll stay long enough to see what's in there."

Owen crept through the gates and darted into the dark shadow by the factory wall. The two other boys quickly followed. They waited, listening for any sound, but all was silent.

"There must be a door somewhere," muttered Owen.

The three began to creep along the factory wall, keeping their heads below the windows. Owen felt his way along the rough brickwork hoping his hands would find a door frame or an opening. But there was nothing.

Owen stopped and Freddie, following, bumped into him.

"What did you do that for?" hissed Freddie.

"Quiet, I'm thinking."

"Can we go home now? It's cold," whispered Chaz.

"You can if you like, but I'm staying 'til I find out what's in there."

Just then the boys heard the sound of an engine and, whizzing through the gates, came the large, black shape of a lorry. The three boys froze. As the lorry's headlights swung across them Owen saw something right next to where he stood.

A ramp.

And above the ramp he saw a metal plate in the wall.

The lorry rumbled away into the shadows.

"Come on," whispered Owen.

Carefully he edged forward and climbed the ramp. He ran his hands over the smooth metal searching for a handle. But there did not seem to be one. He leaned back against the wall disappointed. As he did so he felt something dig into his back. There was a whirring noise, a thin line of blue light glowed for a second around the metal plate . . . and it slid away.

Chapter 3
Tin Can Alley

Owen, Freddie and Chaz stepped inside and found themselves in a small room. On the floor was a pile of packing cases, a rusty tool box and a reel of wire.

"There's nothing here. Can we go now?" whispered Chaz.

"We're in now. Come on. Follow me," said Owen.

On one wall of the room was another metal plate and next to it Owen could see a small, red button. He pressed it, there was a faint hiss, a door slid open and they all stepped out into a corridor. Pipes hung along the ceiling and across the walls. A single red painted line ran down the middle of a grey floor. There was a faint hum from somewhere nearby. Following the red line they set off, no one saying anything. Soon the boys found themselves on a metal walkway high above an enormous room.

"Wow," whispered Chaz, "you could fit twenty football pitches in here."

"Not unless you cleared this lot out first, though," said Freddie.

Packed high to the ceiling were rows and rows of tin cans.

"Look at the labels," gasped Owen, "they're just like my one."

"So, it's a can factory. Can we go home now?" whined Chaz.

"What if someone comes?" said Freddie.

"I've not seen enough yet," said Owen.

At the end of the walkway was a spiral staircase. Owen headed for it and the two boys followed. Carefully they made their way downwards, trying not to make a sound on the metal steps.

Still no one came.

At the bottom they gazed up at the stacked tin cans towering to the ceiling like so many metal sky-scrapers.

"Come on," whispered Owen, "let's see if they are all the same."

He set off down one alleyway between a wall of cans. It was like walking down a road in a big city. Every tin can was the same. The same black label with the words . . .

GREEN SOUP

"Why would anyone want so much soup," said Chaz aloud.

"That's a very good question," said a voice.

And a powerful beam of light flicked on.

Chapter 4
Von Straub

The spotlight shone straight at the visitors so that they could not see. Two giant shadows appeared on the wall. One belonged to Freddie and one to Chaz.

"Where's Owen?" hissed Freddie.

"He was here a second ago."

"Well that's great. He got us into this mess...and now he's scarpered."

"Turn around and come this way," said the voice.

Freddie and Chaz did as they were told. From behind a pillar Owen peeped out, straining to see who the voice belonged to.

"Come closer and let me see who my visitors are." It was a man's voice. It sounded tinny and whining as if it was amplified through a microphone that did not work very well.

The light was turned away and there, standing on a small platform, was a man in a grubby, white coat. He was no taller than either of the boys; his head was entirely hairless except for two large, bushy eyebrows which sprouted above dark, beady eyes.

"So, why have you come here?"

"We didn't mean any harm," began Chaz.

"Yes, we'll be going now. Nice to meet you."

"I don't **sink** so," snarled the little man, in an accent the boys did not recognise.

He turned and flicked a switch behind him. The dark wall behind him suddenly lit up with hundreds of tiny bulbs, buttons, and computer screens.

"My name is Boris Von Straub, and now you shall see my little plan."

Von Straub placed his hand on a joy-stick. There was a faint rumbling and what looked like a giant mechanical arm on wheels appeared. The little man operated the joystick and the arm reached up and took one tin can from the shelf.

"Now you will see my brilliant invention. Soon I will flood the supermarkets with these beauties. Soon there will be one of these in every house in this town."

"He wants to give everyone soup?" whispered Chaz.

"Now see...this is what I have planned for years...ever since they wouldn't let me carry on at that stupid science laboratory. Now they will see. Now they will pay for their mistake."

Von Straub operated the joystick. A lever turned, the can spun around and a circle of tin dropped away. There was a faint hiss and green liquid bubbled over the rim of the can.

"We've seen this trick before," whispered Freddie. But they were not prepared for what came next. A can seemed to grow from inside the first one. Then another . . . and another, in a blur of speed; sometimes in a single column, sometimes two together. Then, just as quickly as it began, it stopped. And something stepped from the empty can.

Chapter 5
"Awake, my Beauties!"

Owen looked on from high up on the walkway. He had stayed behind the pillar all this time. There was no point in all three being captured. It was up to him now.

He had watched horrified as the little man in the white coat had appeared. And then as the can opened and something stepped out; something shaped like a man but made entirely from cans; a tin man that walked, moved its fingers . . . and blinked its eye.

A tin-can robot.

Von Straub was speaking again. "Here it is, my greatest invention. With this robot I can take over this whole city in a single day." He leaned forward to take a closer look at the robot. "That's funny! This one appears to be missing an eye. Never mind. A slight imperfection, that's all."

"But how can one robot take over a city," asked Freddie.

"One? Do you think I have only one?" Von Straub put his head back and laughed. He pointed, wildly. "There, can't you see? There is a robot waiting to be born in every tin can. And soon you will all awake, my beauties!"

"But what do you mean?" spluttered Chaz.

"Are you as stupid as you look?" sneered the little man. "Then let me explain. Tonight, hundreds of lorries will send these harmless looking cans of soup into every supermarket in this city. Soon they will be in every house and home. Then, as the foolish people open them, my robots will appear. I will take control. The city will be mine!" Again his high-pitched laugh echoed around the building.

"So that's it," thought Owen. "And it's up to me to stop him."

Chapter 6
Robot Attack!

Owen knew that there was no time to fetch help. Below him Freddie and Chaz still stood, terrified.

"And now," Von Straub was saying, "you have seen too much already. You cannot leave this building."

"Why not?" stuttered Chaz.

"Please let us go. We won't tell, honest," said Freddie.

"It is too late," sneered the little man.

"RUN!" yelled Owen from the walkway above.

For a split second Von Straub looked up. It was enough.

"Run," yelled Freddie, and the two boys turned and sped off down one of the aisles.

"You won't get away," yelled the little man. "There's nowhere to hide."

Freddie and Chaz hurtled towards the end of the aisle and turned to see not one, but three robots clanking after them.

"Quick, this way," said Chaz, and they turned the next corner to run back up the

next gangway. It was like a giant game of cat and mouse.

Owen suddenly remembered the storeroom. He rushed back along the metal walkway as fast as he could, no longer worrying about the noise his feet made. There was no time for that.

There, still lying on the floor was what he was looking for. The reel of wire. Owen picked it up, already forming a plan in his mind. Racing back along the walkway he could see that the robots had split up and were searching for his friends from different directions.

"Clever robots, too!" he murmured.

"Stop right there," called a voice.

Owen looked up. Standing at the other end of the metal walkway was Von Straub.

"It's no use. You can't escape."

Owen looked around in a panic. The only staircase stood behind the little scientist. There was no other way down . . . unless! Owen looked over the edge. The walkway had to be supported by something. Just next to where he stood was a round, steel pillar.

"I've seen fireman do this on the telly," thought Owen, "but it's a long way down."

But there was no time to wait. Owen

swung himself over the edge, wrapped his arms about the pole and whizzed towards the ground. The mad scientist let out a howl of rage. But then it was Owen's turn to cry out as he looked below him. There was a robot standing at the bottom of the pillar.

There was a loud clank as Owen landed with all his weight on the robot. Bits of metal flew everywhere.

"Not so clever after all," said Owen, to the heap of metal on the floor.

Picking himself up Owen set off, heading for the end of the nearest aisle. There he bent down and unwound one end of the wire. He carefully looped it around the

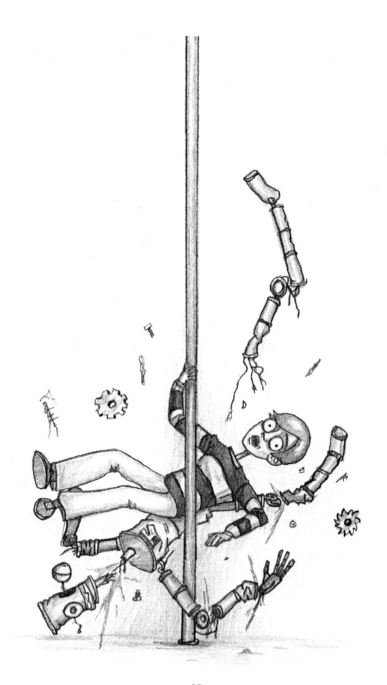

last can at the very bottom corner of the stack.

"I just hope this works!" he muttered to himself.

Then he walked quickly backwards, unrolling the wire as he went.

"Owen!" It was Freddie and Chaz. The two remaining robots would not be far behind.

Owen did not wait but carried on unwinding. He had now reached the middle of the aisle. And the wire ran out.

Owen stooped down and made a large loop of wire, tying it tightly in a knot. He stood up and carefully eased two cans from higher up the stack, taking care not to disturb any others. It worked. He put the two cans on the floor and rested the wire loop so that it was just off the ground. Then the two robots appeared at one end of the gangway.

Owen stood up. "Yah, come and get us, stupid robots!"

The robots hissed green steam from a hole somewhere in their faces. And they began to run towards the boys.

"Come on. Let's get out of here," said Owen.

The three boys ran and reached the staircase just as there was a loud clank. One

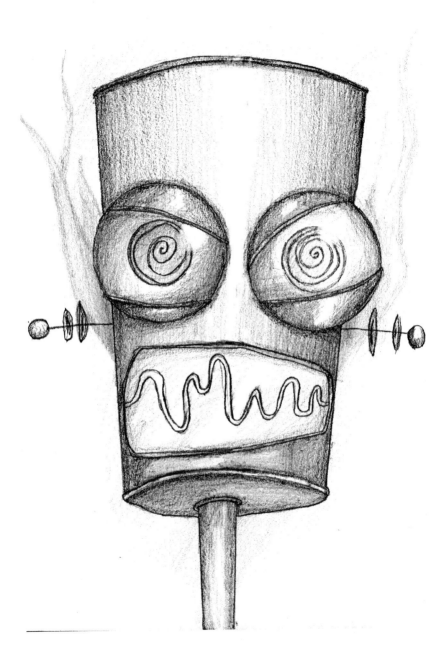

of the robots had caught his foot in the wire loop and was tugging at it hard, trying to free itself.

"Up the stairs. Hurry!" yelled Owen. There was the sound of a single clunk as one can fell away from the stack . . . and then a sound like thunder as other cans began to tumble. The boys raced upwards, found the doorway and were soon gulping in the cold evening air. Behind them the noise of exploding cans was deafening.

Several police-cars stood in the yard having been alerted by the noise. The boys waited at the gate, breathing hard as, eventually, Von Straub staggered out into the darkness, and was quickly led away by four policemen.

. . . .

Back home Owen crept in and closed the door quietly behind him.

His mum called out from somewhere in the kitchen. "Is that you Owen? What have you been up to?"

"Oh, nothing, Mum. Just saving the world from killer robots."

"That's nice, dear. Now go and wash your hands."

Owen could just hear the sound of a can opener whirring in the kitchen.

"It's soup for tea!"

"Oh no . . . !"

Magut the Alien

Chapter One
Aliens in my Shed

The Mars probe has safely landed on the surface of the Red Planet. Scientists are closely studying pictures for signs of life on our closest neighbouring planet. So far there is nothing yet to suggest intelligent life forms of any kind. This is disappointing news for the scientists . . .

Ellis turned off the television and picked up his model spaceship. "Mother-ship to Earth. Landing gear at the ready. Warp factor nine, transmission locked on. Coming in at 1000 miles an hour."

So there were no aliens on Mars. But Ellis knew they were out there somewhere.

When they did eventually come it would just be his luck to miss them anyway. He would be out buying shoes with his mum or something. Anyway, they would probably arrive on the lawn at The White House, or touch down in front of Buckingham Palace. No self respecting alien would come looking for No 3, Wilmington Terrace.

"Ellis, come on, your dinner's nearly ready!"

WHOOSH!

CRASH!

CRUMP!

Something was going on in the garden. Ellis went to the window, pulled back the curtain, and looked out.

Someone had stolen the shed roof!

"Ellis, come and get your burgers. They'll be cold soon."

"Coming. I'm just washing my hands."

Ellis went to the door that led through to the garage. From here you could get out into the garden without being seen. He closed the door quietly behind him and made his way past the jumble of paint pots, old furniture and tools that cluttered the garage walls. Then, taking the shed key from its hook, he went out into the garden.

Ellis blinked and rubbed his eyes. There was the shed. And the roof was back!

He was just about to unlock the padlock when he noticed something.

There was a green light coming from under the door!

Chapter Two
"Greetings Earthchild!"

There was something in there.

Ellis stopped still, hardly daring to breathe. There was a faint noise, a rhythmic, humming sound coming from inside.

Carefully, Ellis turned the key in the old lock, the padlock opened and Ellis undid the latch. The door opened slightly and the green light seeped out into the gloom of an autumn evening.

Now the sound could be heard more clearly . . . a steady, throbbing, rhythmic hum, like the sound you get when you stand under an electricity pylon on a wet day.

Ellis took a deep breath and stepped inside.

Standing right in the middle of the potting shed was a spaceship. It was like nothing Ellis had ever seen before, but there could be no doubt that it was a spaceship.

As spaceships go it was not enormous, but it filled the potting shed.

The strange craft was shaped like a pointed dome. It gleamed a metallic silver colour and, on four sides, were placed

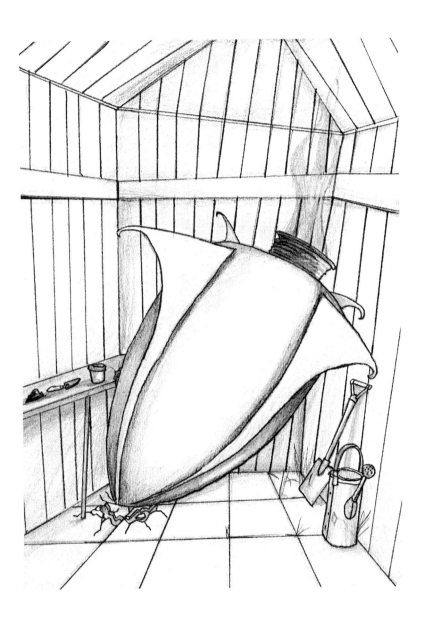

triangular wings reaching nearly to the top. Underneath the dome a green light glowed and pulsed, almost as if somewhere inside a heart was beating.

There was something missing.

"No doors or windows!" Ellis whispered.

Then, as if responding to his words, a door opened. It did not so much open as grow a hole where the side of the ship had been. And, just as quickly as it had appeared, it grew shut again.

"Greetings Earthchild!" said a voice.

Chapter Three
Magut

Ellis looked straight ahead. He had not seen anyone appear from the ship. He felt sweat break out on the back of his neck, and begin to run inside his collar. Was there an invisible alien in the shed?

There was crackle of electric noise like the hissing of a radio being tuned to a channel.

"Greetings Earthchild. I come in . . . zeeblework . . . I come in peas . . . Blast . . . grumble fange . . . blatter . . ."

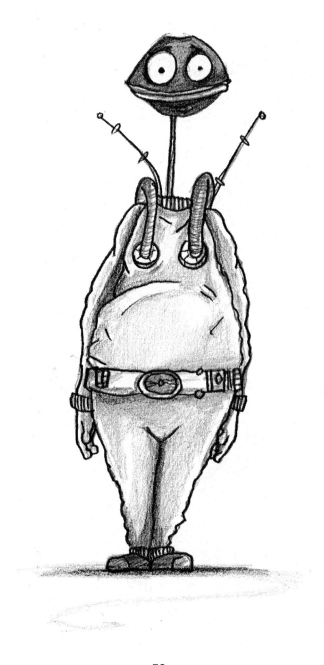

Ellis looked down. Between his feet there was an alien.

It was about twice the height of the green watering-can it stood beside, and about the same colour. Its head was dome-shaped, like the ship; its face resembled a green potato with two eyes and rubbery purple lips, but no sign of a nose or ears; from head to foot it wore a shimmering, green space-suit from which sprouted strange tubes of a bluish liquid.

"Who are you?" asked Ellis.

The alien fiddled with a dial on his belt and the electric noise began again.

"My name is Margaret . . . No, no, that's not right!"

More electric noise.

"Beeble . . . .box . . . fagglewarpblaster . . . voice modulator not working . . . Oh, it is now!"

The alien gave a cough, cleared his tubes, and started again.

"My name is Magut.   Is this your planet?"

Chapter Four
New Shoes

"Ellis, I'm not telling you again! Come and get your dinner."

"I've got to go."

"Who is this that commands you?" asked Magut the Alien.

"It's my mum. She's indoors and she's cross."

"Can I journey with you to My Mum?"

"No, you'd better stay here. I'll come back for you later."

Ellis shut the door behind him and snapped the padlock shut, then ran inside the house. Mum had nearly finished her dinner as Ellis sat down.

"I don't know why I bother cooking your food. You might as well eat it straight from the freezer," said his mum, "It's always cold by the time you get here."

"Sorry," mumbled Ellis between mouthfuls of burger.

"Anyway, we've got to go into town to get you some new shoes."

Ellis groaned.

"It's no use complaining! You can't go to school in those." She pointed to her son's feet. "They're nearly falling to bits."

. . . .

The shoe shop was jammed with people; shop assistants were carrying armfuls of boxes, harassed mums were clutching toddlers; in the doorway stood a charity box in the shape of a plastic alien.

"What about these, Love?"

Ellis looked at the brown leather lace-ups and made a face.

"I like the ones that look like trainers," said Ellis.

"Well, they're not suitable for school. You'll just have to have these," said Mum.

"I'll put them in the box for you," said the assistant.

"But I don't want them," said Ellis.
Mum was not taking any notice,

Then Ellis turned towards the doorway.
A boy was trying to put some money into the
alien in the shop doorway.

Suddenly the boy thumped the top of
the charity box. And then the boy vanished.
One second he was there and then he was
gone. Ellis looked hard. Suddenly the plastic
alien looked very familiar.

Magut!

Then the lady came back with the shoe
box. She put it on the chair beside Ellis.

"I'll go and get you a carrier bag," she
smiled.

65

Ellis looked down at the box and it vanished. The assistant returned.

"What have you done with the box?" said Mum, accusingly.

"I haven't done anything."

The shop assistant looked everywhere but the shoes were nowhere to be seen.

"Come on, we'll have the ones with the blue stripe. Let's just get home."

When they arrived back at the car park there was a traffic warden standing by the car.

The traffic warden was peeling a ticket from his pad.

"But we're only a minute late," said Mum, looking at her watch.

Then the ticket on the windscreen disappeared. And then the traffic warden vanished too.

Mum blinked and looked at Ellis.

"It's nothing to do with me," said Ellis.

"Come on, let's get home before anything else happens," said Mum.

"This is great," thought Ellis, "my alien can get rid of anything and anyone I don't like. Fantastic!"

Chapter Five
Happy Birthday!

"Happy Birthday, Ellis"

Waiting to come in were a cowboy and a fairy princess holding enormous presents. It was Mum's idea to have a fancy dress party. Ellis was already in his space suit.

Soon the room was filled with soldiers, fairies, knights in armour and a couple of Robin Hoods.

The table was laid with sandwiches, cakes, crisps and jellies, and there were balloons hung on every wall.

"Let's play Squeak Piggy-Squeak," said Samantha Hills, from somewhere inside a frothy pink dress. The boys and some of the girls groaned.

"What a good idea," said Mum. "Let's start with the birthday boy!"

"Oh no!" moaned Ellis, but it was no good.

The blindfold was put on and Ellis was spun around three times until he was slightly dizzy. Then, stumbling about the room to squeals of laughter, he eventually put his hands on two shoulders.

"Squeak Piggy-Squeak," said Ellis.

"Squeak, Earthchild!" said a voice.

Ellis pulled down the blindfold.

"That's cheating, you're supposed to guess," shrieked Samantha.

There was Magut.

"Hello, Ellis," he said.

"What are you doing here," hissed Ellis, under his breath.

"I've never been to an Earth party," said Magut. "I thought I would see what one was like."

"What a brilliant costume," said Mum. "Did you hire it?"

"It's made from the skin of Zorbs," said Magut.

"Oh, you are funny," said Mum.

All the children crowded round.

"What's that thing?" asked a small child.

"It's a molecular vaporiser."

Magut pointed the transparent tube at a sausage roll . . . and it disappeared.

"Hooray! Do some more magic!" shouted the children.

"Later," said Ellis, turning pale. The party continued.

Magut was a great hit. He let the children play pin-the-tail-on-the-alien. He memorised every single thing on the memory-tray. He won hunt the thimble by making it completely vanish.

Then it was time for food.

Everyone sat down. Children piled their plates high with sandwiches, crisps and cakes. Magut joined in.

Happy Birthday to you . . .

Round the corner came Mum, carrying the birthday cake

Happy Birthday to you . . .

The cake had ten candles on it, the sort that fizzed and sparkled when they were lit.

Happy Birthday dear Ellis.

"Aaargh!" Magut suddenly stood up, his eyes widening at the lighted candles. "Attack, attack. Prepare to fire."

And then the cake disappeared.

And then Mum vanished too.

Chapter Six
Life on Mars

"You've vaporised my Mum," Ellis shouted.

Samantha Hills began to cry.

Some aliens really knew how to spoil a party.

When everyone had gone home Ellis sat Magut down on the settee.

"What's happened to my mum?"

"I'm sorry, Ellis," said Magut. "I thought we were being attacked."

"By a birthday cake? How are we going to get her back?" Ellis wailed.

"Oh that's not difficult" said Magut. "We just need a Particle Re-structuriser."

"Have you got one?"

"Yes."

"Where?"

"On my planet."

Still wearing his space suit Ellis ran to the shed with Magut.

The door grew open and they both stepped inside the ship. On every wall there were lights and buttons and two seats were positioned by a large screen. Magut tapped a

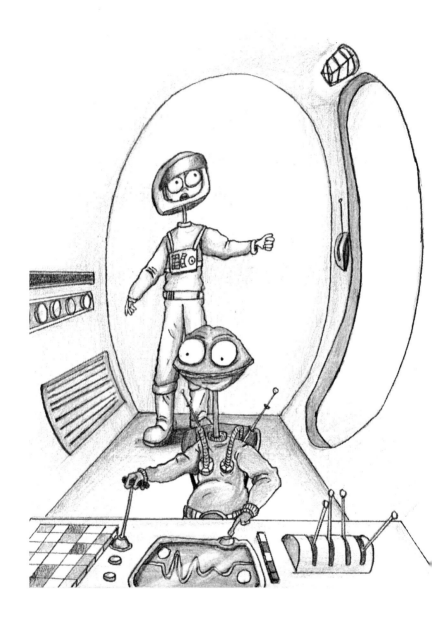

few keys in front of him and the screen flickered into life.

"Blast," he said, "the launch-clearway device is jammed."

"What does that mean?" asked Ellis.

"It just means that we'll have to take your dad's potting shed with us," said the alien, frowning. "Do you think he'll notice? "9...8...7...6...5...4...3 Blast off!"

"What happened to 2 and 1?" asked Ellis.

"These spaceships aren't as accurate as they used to be," replied Magut.

The ground began to move, the ship began to shake violently and then they were pinned back in their seats as the ship accelerated upwards.

Next door's cat hissed loudly and scuttled under the fence as the shed lifted into the sky.

"How long before we reach Mars?"

"About five and a half of your Earth minutes. Sorry it takes so long!"

Soon the glowing outline of the Red Planet came into view on the screen.

"Are you the only alien here?" asked Ellis. "Only, no one has ever seen anything on the surface of Mars."

"That's because we're not on the

surface," replied Magut. "We're underneath it. Now, fasten your belts. We're coming in."

There was a slight bump as they touched down.

Ellis watched the wall where the door had opened before but, instead, a hole grew open at his feet.

"Come on," said Magut.

Following the alien, Ellis slid down a long tube, coming out into a large underground chamber. Here there were more aliens, just like Magut. Strange plants grew on the ceiling and rows of computer screens lined the walls.

Magut led them along a corridor to another room. This room was empty except

for a giant, transparent tube right in the middle. Magut placed his hand on the wall and a panel grew open to reveal more dials and switches. The alien fiddled with a dial and a pair of brown shoes appeared inside the tube. The tube revolved once and the shoes tumbled out.

Then a birthday cake appeared.

Then a small boy holding a penny.

Then a traffic warden.

And then Ellis's mum.

"Now we must return you to Earth. My ship will take you."

Scientists have finally discovered evidence that there may be life on Mars. The Mars probe is even now sending amazing pictures back to Earth. We can go live, by satellite, to the command centre now.

Mum looked up from her ironing to watch the news.

A blurred image slowly appeared on the screen.

Dad put down his paper to watch too.

The image began to clear.

Ellis blinked at the screen and rubbed his eyes.

The picture showed the red surface of a strange planet.

And there, standing between two craters, was . . .

a garden shed.